Alfred Wiedemann

The Ancient Egyptian Doctrine of the Immortality of the Soul

Alfred Wiedemann

The Ancient Egyptian Doctrine of the Immortality of the Soul

ISBN/EAN: 9783337228033

Printed in Europe, USA, Canada, Australia, Japan

Cover: Foto ©Andreas Hilbeck / pixelio.de

More available books at **www.hansebooks.com**

THE

ANCIENT EGYPTIAN DOCTRINE

OF THE

IMMORTALITY OF THE SOUL

BY

ALFRED WIEDEMANN, D.PH.

PROFESSOR OF ORIENTAL LANGUAGES AT THE UNIVERSITY OF BONN

AUTHOR OF

" ÆGYPTISCHE GESCHICHTE," " DIE RELIGION DER ALTEN ÆGYPTER,"
" HERODOT'S ZWEITES BUCH "

With Twenty-one Illustrations

LONDON

H. GREVEL & CO.

33, KING STREET, COVENT GARDEN, W.C.

1895

PREFACE.

IN writing this treatise my object has been to give a clear exposition of the most important shape which the doctrine of immortality assumed in Egypt. This particular form of the doctrine was only one of many different ones that were held. The latter, however, were but occasional manifestations, whereas the system here treated of was the popular belief among all classes of the Egyptian people, from early to Coptic times. By far the greater part of the religious papyri and tomb texts and of the inscriptions of funerary stelæ are devoted to it; the symbolism of nearly all the amulets is connected with it; it was bound up with the practice of mummifying the dead; and it centred in the person of Osiris, the most popular of all the gods of Egypt.

Even in Pyramid times Osiris had already attained pre-eminence; he maintained this position throughout the whole duration of Egyptian national life, and even survived its fall. From the fourth century B.C. he, together with his companion deities, entered into the religious life of the Greeks; and homage was paid to him by imperial Rome. Throughout the length and breadth of the Roman Empire, even to the remotest provinces of the Danube and the Rhine, altars were raised to him, to his wife Isis, and to his son Harpocrates; and wherever his worship spread, it carried with it that doctrine of immortality which was associated with his name. This Osirian doctrine influenced the systems of Greek philosophers; it made itself felt in the teachings of the Gnostics; we find traces of it in the writings of Christian apologists and the older fathers of the Church, and through their agency it has affected the thoughts and opinions of our own time.

The cause of this far-reaching influence lies both in the doctrine itself, which was at once the most profound and the most attractive of all the teachings of the Egyptian religion; and also in the comfort and consolation to be derived from the pathetically human story of its founder, Osiris. He, the son of the gods, had sojourned upon earth and bestowed upon men the blessings of civilisation. At length he fell a prey to the devices of the Wicked One, and was slain. But the triumph of evil and of death was only apparent : the work of Osiris endured, and his son followed in his footsteps and broke the power of evil. Neither had his being ended with death, for on dying he had passed into the world to come, henceforth to reign over the dead as " The Good Being." Even as Osiris, so must each man die, no matter how noble and how godly his life ; nevertheless his deeds should be established for ever, his name should endure, and the life which is eternal awaited him beyond the tomb. To the Egyptian, nature on every hand presented images of the life of Osiris. To him that life was reflected in the struggle between good and evil, in the contest between the fertilising Nile and the encroaching desert, no less than in the daily and yearly courses of the sun. In earlier times Osiris was occasionally confounded with the Sun god ; later, the two deities

were habitually merged in one another. The death
and resurrection of Osiris occurred at the end of the
month Khoiak—that is to say, at the winter solstice,
concurrently with the dying of the Sun of the Old
Year and the rising of the Sun of the New. The
new phœnix was supposed to make his appearance in March; and this bird, although usually
associated with the Sun, was often representative
of Osiris. And the epithets and titles of the Sun
god were similarly bestowed upon Osiris.

All the Osirian doctrines were readily apprehended
in spite of their deep import, and they steadily tended
towards the evolution of a high form of monotheistic
belief. To no close student of these doctrines can
the fact seem strange that Egypt should have been
the first country in which Christianity permeated the
whole body of the people. The Egyptian could
recognise his old beliefs in many a Christian theme,
and so much did the figure of Christ remind him
of Osiris and his son Horus, that to him Christ
became a hero who traversed the Nile valley even
as Horus had done, overcoming His enemies, the
evil demons and the wicked. In Egypt the Osirian

faith and dogma were the precursors of Christianity, the foundations upon which it was able to build ; and, altogether apart from their intrinsic worth and far-reaching influence, it is this which constitutes their significance in the history of the world.

For the choice of the illustrations, as well as for the English version, I am gratefully indebted to my translator.

ALFRED WIEDEMANN.

Bonn, *March* 1895.

THE

ANCIENT EGYPTIAN DOCTRINE

OF THE

IMMORTALITY OF THE SOUL.

L ITTLE as we know of the ancient Egyptian
religion in its entirety, and of its motley
mixture of childishly crude fetichism and deep
philosophic thought, of superstition and true religious
worship, of polytheism, henotheism, and pantheism,
one dogma stands out clearly from this confusion,
one article of belief to which the Egyptian religion
owes its unique position among all other religions
of antiquity—the doctrine of the immortality of the
human soul. It is true that other ancient religions
attained to a similar dogma, for the belief was
early developed among Semites, Indo-germanians,

Turanians, and Mongolians ; but in all these cases it appears as the outcome of a higher conception of man and God and of their reciprocal relationship, and, when attained to, brought about the abandonment of grossly material forms of thought. But in Egypt we have the unique spectacle of one of the most elaborated forms of the doctrine of immortality side by side with the most elementary conception of higher beings ever formulated by any people. We do not know whether the belief in immortality which prevailed in the valley of the Nile is as old as the Egyptian religion in general, although at first sight it appears to be so. The oldest of the longer religious texts which have come down to us are found in the wall inscriptions of pyramids of kings of the Fifth and Sixth Dynasties (according to Manetho's scheme of the dynasties), and must be dated to at least 3000 B.C. In these texts the doctrine of immortality appears as a completed system with a long history of development behind it.

In that system, all the stages through which this doctrine of the Egyptian religion had successively passed are preserved ; for the Egyptians were so immoderately conservative in everything that they could not make up their minds to give up their old ideas of deity, even after having advanced to higher and purer ones. The older ideas were all carefully retained, and we find various systems of religion which in point of time had followed each other on Egyptian soil afterwards existing side by side. There is no trace of any struggle for the victory between these systems ; each new order of thought was taken as it arose into the circle of the older ones, however heterogeneous it might be to the rest. The consequence was that in Egypt there was no religious progress in our sense of the term. With us it is essential that old and outworn forms of belief should be cast off; with them a new doctrine could achieve no greater success than to win a place among the older conceptions of the Egyptian Pantheon.

Each single divinity, each religious belief, each amulet, has in itself a clear and intelligible significance ; and where this is apparently otherwise it is not because the point was obscure to the Egyptian mind, but because we have not yet succeeded in making it clear to ourselves. When we abandon the consideration of single points and try to imagine how the different detached notions were combined by the people into one belief, and what picture they had really formed of their Heaven and Pantheon—then we have set ourselves an impossible task. Many divinities have precisely the same character and perform the same functions; whole circles of ideas are mutually exclusive; yet all existed together and were accepted and believed in at one and the same time.

In these circumstances any discussion of Egyptian religious ideas must begin by dealing with isolated facts; each divinity, each idea, each smallest amulet must be carefully examined by itself and treated of in the light of the texts specially referring to it. Generations of Egyptians pondered on each single point seeking to elucidate it. With anxious fear priests and laymen strove to acquire the use of all the formulæ by the help of which man hoped to appease the gods, overcome demons, and attain to bliss, and all sought to provide themselves with every amulet possessing efficacy for the world to come and import for man's eternal welfare. But great as must have been the expenditure of thought which produced and developed their various religious doctrines, the Egyptians never succeeded in welding their different beliefs and practices into one consistent whole.

In most religions the gods of life are distinct from

the gods of death, but such a distinction scarcely existed at all in Egypt. There the same beings who were supposed to determine the fate of man in this world were supposed to determine it also in the world to come; only in the case of certain deities sometimes the one and sometimes the other side of the divine activity was brought into special prominence. The exercise of their different functions by the gods was not in accordance with any fixed underlying principle, was not any essential outcome of their characters, but rather a matter of their caprice and inclination. In course of time the Egyptian idea of these functions changed, and was variously apprehended in different places. It seems to us at first as though the relation of the gods to the life beyond had nearly everywhere been regarded as more important than their relation to this life. But this impression is owing to the fact that our material for the study of the Egyptian religion is almost exclusively derived from tombs and funerary temples, while the number of Egyptian monuments unconnected with the cult of the dead is comparatively small.

On this account it has been supposed that both in their religion and in their public life the Egyptians turned all their thoughts towards death and what lay beyond it. But a close examination of the monuments has proved that they had as full an enjoyment of the life here as other nations of antiquity, and that they are not to be regarded as a stiff and spiritless race of men whose thoughts were pedantically turned towards the contemplation of the next world.

Had this been the case, the Egyptians would have come to hold a pessimistic view of the life here and hereafter something like that prevailing in India, and have striven to escape from the monotony and dulness of existence by seeking some means to end it. But this is the reverse of what happened in the valley of the Nile. The most ardent wish of its inhabitants was to remain on earth as long as possible, to attain to the age of one hundred and ten years, and to continue to lead after death the same life which they had been wont to lead while here. They pictured the after-life in the most material fashion ; they could imagine no fairer existence than that which they led on the banks of the Nile. How simple and at the same time how complicated were their conceptions can best be shown by some account of their ideas on the immortality of the soul and its constitution as a combination of separate parts set forth in ancient Egyptian documents.

When once a man was dead, when his heart had ceased to beat and warmth had left his body, a lifeless hull was all that remained of him upon earth. The first duty of the survivors was to preserve this from destruction, and to that end it was handed over to a guild whose duty it was to carry out its embalment under priestly supervision. This was done according to old and strictly established rules. The internal and more corruptible parts were taken away, and the rest of the body—*i.e.*, the bony framework and its covering—was soaked in natron and asphalt, smeared with sweet-smelling unguents, and made incorruptible. The inside of the body was filled with linen bandaging and asphalt, among which were placed all kinds of amulets symbolising immortality—heart-shaped vases, snake-heads in carnelian, scarabæi, and little glazed-ware figures of divinities. By their mystic power these amulets were intended to further and assist the preservation of the corpse, for which physical provision had already been made by embalmment. In about seventy days, when the work of embalmment was completed, the body was wrapped in linen bandages, placed in a coffin, and so returned to the family.

The friends and relatives of the deceased then

carried the dead in solemn procession across the river to his last resting-place, which he had provided for himself in the hills forming the western boundary of the valley of the Nile. Mourning-women accompanied the procession with their wailing ; priests burnt incense and intoned prayers, and other priests made offerings and performed mysterious ceremonies both during the procession and at the entrance to the tomb.* The mummy was then lowered into the vault, which was closed and walled up, further offerings were made, and afterwards the mourners partook of the funeral feast in the ante-chamber of the tomb. Harpers were there who sang of the dead man and of his worth, and exhorted his relations to forget their grief and again to rejoice in life, so long as it should be granted unto them

---

* The whole process of embalmment is briefly described in the *Rhind Papyrus*, edited by BIRCH, London, 1863, and by BRUGSCH, Leipzig, 1865. The procedure of the *taricheuts* is described in a Vienna papyrus, edited by BERGMANN, Vienna, 1887, and the conclusion of their operations in a Paris papyrus and a Bûlaq papyrus, edited by MASPERO, *Pap. du Louvre*, Paris, 1875. For the transport of the mummy, see DÜMICHEN, *Kal. Insch.*, pl. 35 *sqq*. The minutely ordered ritual for the ceremonies at the door of the tomb was published and investigated in SCHIAPARELLI's admirable work, *Il Libro dei Funerali*, Turin, 1881—1890.

to enjoy the light of the sun ; for when life is past
man knows not what shall follow it ; beyond the
grave is darkness and long sleep.　Gayer and gayer
grew the banquet, often degenerating into an orgy ;
when at length all the guests had withdrawn, the
tomb was closed, and the dead was left alone.
Afterwards it was only on certain feast days that
the relatives made pilgrimages to the city of the
dead, sometimes alone and sometimes accompanied
by priests.　On these occasions they again entered
the ante-chamber of the tomb, and there offered
prayers to the dead, or brought him offerings,
either in the shape of real foods and drinks,
or else under the symbolic forms of little clay
models of oxen, geese, cakes of bread, and the
like.　Otherwise the tomb remained unvisited.　How
it there fared with the dead could only be learned
from the doctrines and mysteries of religion ; to
descend into the vault and disturb the peace of
the mummy was accounted a heavy crime against
both gods and men.

And yet how much an Egyptian could have wished
to look behind the sealed walls of the sepulchral
chamber and see what secret and mysterious things
there befell the dead !　For their existence had not

terminated with death ; their earthly being only
had come to an end, but they themselves had
entered on a new, a higher and an eternal life. The
constituent parts, whose union in the man had made
a human life possible, separated at the moment of
his death into those which were immortal and those
which were mortal. But while the latter formed
a unity, and constituted the corruptible body
only (KHA), on which the above-mentioned
rites of embalmment were practised, each of the
former were distinct even when in combination.
These "living, indestructible" parts of a man, which
together almost correspond to our idea of the soul,
had found their common home in his living body ;
but on leaving it at his death each set out alone
to find its own way to the gods. If all succeeded
in doing so, and it was further proved that the
deceased had been good and upright, they again
became one with him, and so entered into the
company of the blessed, or even of the gods.

The most important of all these component parts *

* On these component parts cf. WIEDEMANN in the *Proceedings of the Orientalist Congress at St. Etienne*, II. (1878), p. 159
et seq. Many parallel texts to the additional chapter of *The Book
of the Dead*, there referred to, may be found in VON BERGMANN's
Sarkophag des Panehemisis, I., p. 22; II., p. 74 *et seq.*

was the so-called ⎿⎦, KA, the divine counterpart of the deceased, holding the same relation to him as a word to the conception which it expresses, or a statue to the living man. It was his individuality as embodied in the man's name; the picture of him which was, or might have been, called up in the minds of those who knew him at the mention of that name.* Among other races similar thoughts have given rise to higher ideas, and led to a philosophic explanation of the distinction between personalities and persons, such as that contained in the Platonic Ideas. But the Egyptian was incapable of abstract thought, and was reduced to forming a purely concrete conception of this individuality, which is strangely impressive by reason of its thorough sensuousness. He endowed it with a material form completely corresponding to that of the man, exactly resembling him, his second self, his Double, his *Doppelgänger.*†

Many scenes, dating from the eighteenth century

* On this account KA was sometimes used as interchangeable with REN (⌢)—name.

† There is no modern word which exactly expresses the Egyptian idea of the KA; Maspero's translation of " DOUBLE, *Doppelgänger*" is the best hitherto proposed; Meyer's translation of " *Ghost*" (*Gesch. Æg.*, p. 83) is altogether misleading.

B.C. and onwards, represent different kings appearing

Fig. 1.—Hatshepsû, accompanied by her KA, making perfume-
offerings.   (*From the temple of Dêr el Bahri.*) *

* The illustration is taken from LEPSIUS, *Denkmäler*, III. 21.
Here the solar cartouche, or throne-name, of Thothmes II., and his

before divinities, while behind the king stands his
KA, as a little man with the king's features (fig. 1),
or as a staff with two hands (fig. 2),* and surmounted
by certain symbols of royalty, or by the king's head.
In these scenes the Personality accompanies the
Person, following him as a shadow follows a man.

But even as early as the time of Amenophis III.,
about 1500 B.C., the Egyptians had carried the idea
still further, and had completely dissevered the Per-

Horus- or Ka-name, are palimpsests effacing the names of Queen
Hatshepsû Rāmaka, the builder of the temple. The figures in
this scene originally represented the Queen and her KA; but as
she is always portrayed in male attire throughout the temple, it
was only necessary to change her names in order to appropriate
her figure as that of a king. The first satisfactory explanation of
the Horus- or KA-name was given by PETRIE in *A Season in
Egypt*, pp. 21, 22; cf. MASPERO, *Études Égyptologiques*, II.,
p. 273 *et seq*. He shows that the rectangular parallelogram
in which the Horus-name is written is the exact equivalent of
the square panel over the false door in the tomb, by which the
KA was supposed to pass from the sepulchral vault into the
upper chamber, or tomb-chapel, where offerings were provided
for it. A private person had but one name, which was also the
name of his KA. But, on ascending the throne, the king took
four new names in addition to the one which he had hitherto
borne, and among them a name for his KA.

* We have a crude representation of this KA sign, dating from
the reign of Amenemhat I., of the Twelfth Dynasty; see PETRIE,
Tanis I. (Second Memoir of the Egypt Exploration Fund), pl. I.,
No. 3.

sonality from the Person, the king being frequently
represented as appearing before his own Personality,

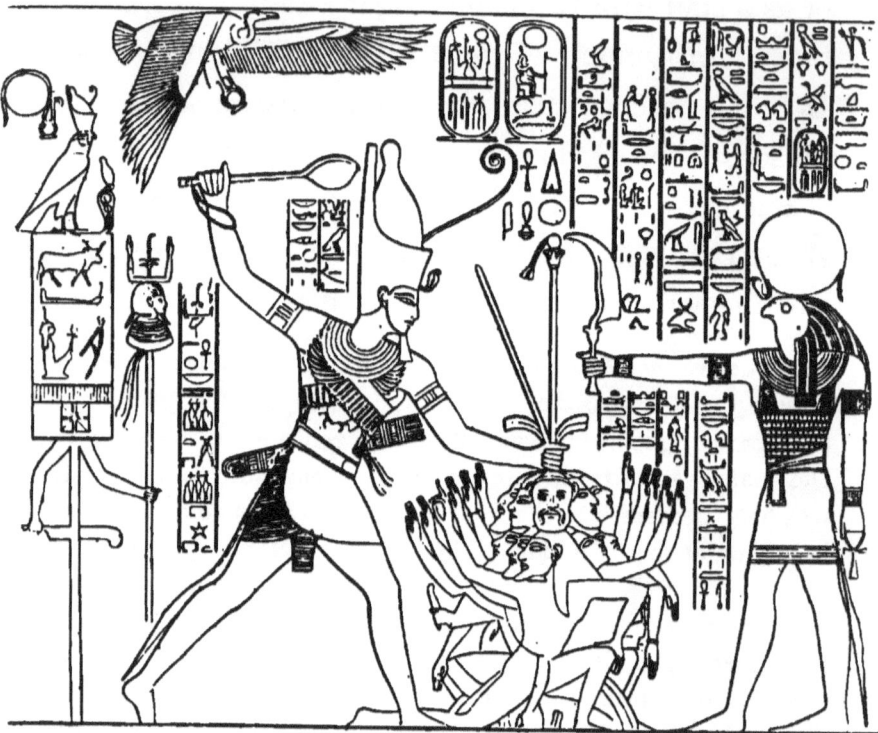

Fig. 2.—The KA of Rameses II., represented by the two-handed staff,
standing behind the king while he slays his enemies before Rā
Harmakhis. (*From Abû Simbel.*) *

which bears the insignia of divinity, the staff of
command, and the symbol of life, the ⚱ *ānkh* (fig. 3).

* LEPSIUS, *Denkmäler*, III. 186. The hands of the KA-
staff have doubtless a common origin with those of the KA-
sign—⊔⊔.

To it the king presents offerings of every kind and
prefers his petition for gifts of the gods in exchange

Fig. 3.—Amenophis III. making offerings to his KA.   (*From his
temple at Soleb.*) *

His Personality replies : "I give unto thee all Life,
all Stability, all Power, all Health, and all Joy
(enlargement of heart) ; I subdue for thee the

* LEPSIUS, *Denkmäler*, III. 87.

peoples of Nubia (Khent), so that thou mayest cut off their heads." In bas-reliefs of the same period which represent the birth of Amenophis III.,* his KA is born at the same time as the king, and both are presented to Amen Rā, as two boys exactly alike (fig. 4), and blessed by him. About this time the kings began to build temples to their own Personalities, and appointed priests to them ; and from time to time the sovereign would visit his temple to implore from himself his own protection, and still greater gifts. So long as the king walked the earth, so long his "living KA, lord of Upper and Lower Egypt, tarried in his dwelling, in the Abode of Splendour (⬚ ⬚ *Pa Dûat*)" ; † for his KA was himself, independent of him, superior to him, and yet his counterpart and bound up with him.

The disjunction of the Personality from the Person was not, however, rigorously and systematically insisted upon ; the two were indeed separate, but were so far one as to come into being only through and with each other. A man lived no longer than

---

* In the course of his excavations at Dêr el Bahri, for the Egypt Exploration Fund, M. Naville discovered the originals of these scenes in a series of bas-reliefs representing the birth of Queen Hatshepsû which were plagiarised by Amenophis III.

† LEPSIUS, *Denkmäler*, III. 21, 129.

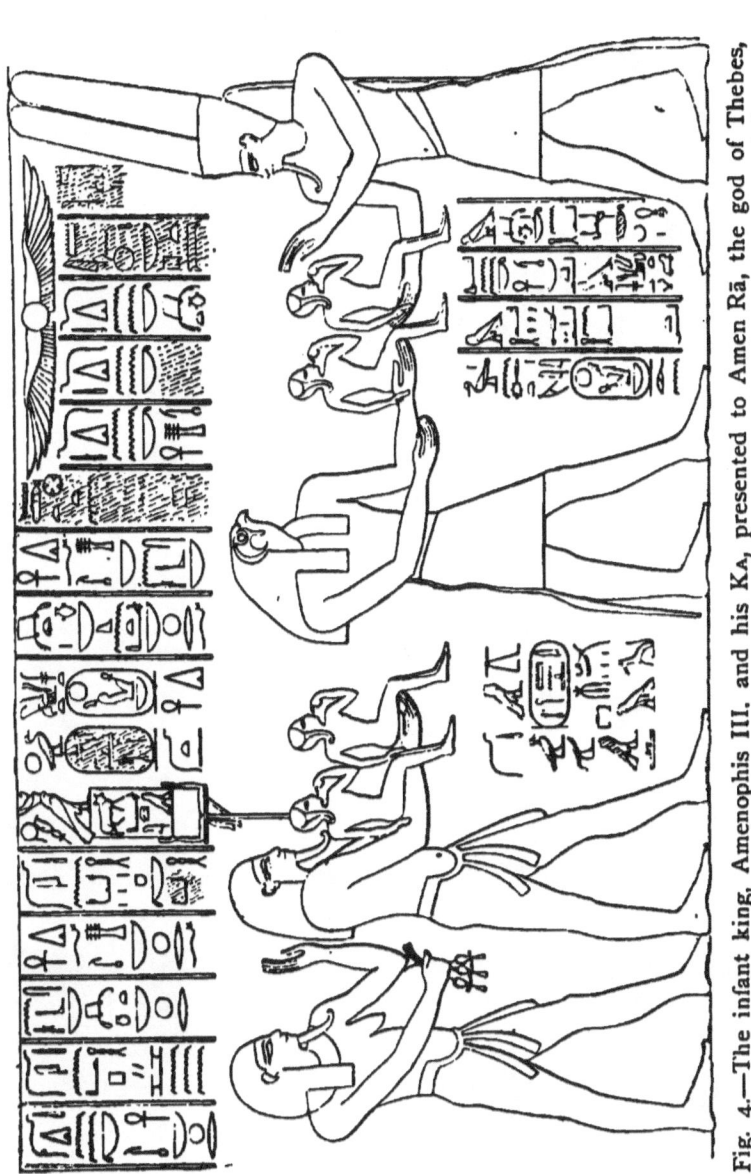

Fig. 4.—The infant king, Amenophis III. and his KA, presented to Amen Rā, the god of Thebes, by two Nile gods, and by Horus. (*From the temple of Amenophis III., at Luxor.*) *

* Lepsius, *Denkmäler*, III., pl. 75.

2

his KA remained with him, and it never left him until the moment of his death. But there was this difference in their reciprocal relations: the KA could live without the body, but the body could not live without the KA. Yet this does not imply that the KA was a higher, a spiritual being; it was material in just the same way as the body itself, needing food and drink for its well-being, and suffering hunger and thirst if these were denied it. In this respect its lot was the common lot of Egyptian gods; they also required bodily sustenance, and were sorely put to it if offerings failed them and their food and drink were unsupplied.

After a man's death his KA became his Personality proper; prayers and offerings were made to the gods that they might grant bread and wine, meat and milk, and all good things needful for the sustenance of a god to the KA of the deceased.*

* Such prayers were also inscribed on funerary stelæ in order that passers-by might repeat them for the benefit of the dead. These inscriptions vary but little. The prayer on the funerary tablet of Khemnekht (now in the Agram Museum) dates from the Thirteenth Dynasty, and runs as follows: "O every scribe, every Kherheb (lector, priestly reciter), all ye who pass by this stele, who love and honour your gods, and would have your offices to flourish (shine) for your children, say ye: 'Let royal offerings be brought unto Osiris for the Ka of the priest

Offerings were also made to the KA itself, and it was believed that from time to time it visited the tomb in order to accept the food there provided for it.   On such occasions it became incorporate in the mummy, which began to live and grow (⊘ 𒑊 ▭ *rûd*), or renew itself as do plants and trees (⊘ ▫ 𝄐 *renp*), and became, as the texts occasionally express it, "the living KA in its coffin." The rich founded endowments whose revenues were to be expended to all time in providing their KAS with food offerings, and bequeathed certain sums for the maintenance of priests to attend to this; large staffs of officials were kept up to provide the necessaries of life for the Personalities of the dead.*

Khemnekht.'"   For an account of the development of the formulæ on funerary stelæ, see WIEDEMANN, *Observations sur quelques stèles funéraires égyptiennes, Le Muséon X.*, 42, 199 *et seq.*

* The particulars above summarised may be verified from contracts which a prince (*erpâ-hâ*) of Siût concluded with the priests of Anubis under the Tenth or Eleventh Dynasty (discussed by MASPERO, *Transactions of the Society of Biblical Archæology*, VII., p. 6 *et seq.*, *Études de Mythologie*, I., p. 62 *et seq.*, and ERMAN, *Æg. Zeitschr.*, 1882, p. 159 ff., the best publication of these inscriptions being that by GRIFFITH, *Inscriptions of Siût and Dêr Rifeh*, London, 1889.   Similar contracts were made even in the times of the pyramid-building kings: cf. *e.g.* LEPSIUS, *Denkmäler*, II. 3-7; DE ROUGÉ, *Inscriptions hiéroglyphiques*, pl. I.; MARIETTE, *Les Mastabahs*, p. 316 *et seq.*)

The KA was represented by statues of the dead
man which were placed within his tomb, and sometimes in temples also by gracious permission of the
sovereign.*   Wherever one of these statues stood,
there might the KA sojourn and take part in Feasts
of Offerings and the pleasures of earthly life; there
even seems to have been a belief that it might be
imprisoned in a statue by means of certain magic
formulæ.   Royal statues in the temples were destined
to the use of the royal KAS, the many statues of
the same king in one temple being apparently all
intended for his own KA service. †

The Egyptians, holding the belief that the statue
of a human being represented and embodied a human
KA, concluded that the statues of the gods represented
and embodied divine KAS, and were indeed neither
more nor less than the KAS of the gods.   Thus the
idea of divinity became entirely anthropomorphic,
and, just as the king built his temple not to himself
but to his Personality, so also sanctuaries were
sometimes dedicated not to a god himself but to

* As in the case of statues found in the temple of Ptah at
Memphis (MARIETTE, *Mon. div.*, pl. 27 b), and in that of Amon at
Karnak (MARIETTE, *Karnak*, pl. 8 f; cf. LEPSIUS, *Auswahl*, pl. 11).

† This striking theory was first broached by MASPERO, *Rec. de
Trav.*, I., p. 154; *Études de Mythologie*, I. p. 80.

his Personality. For example, the chief temple of Memphis was not for the service of the god Ptah, —the maker of the world, whom the Greeks compared to Hephæstos,—but rather for that of his KA. Ptah was not alone among the gods in this respect. The pyramid texts show that even in the times of the Fifth and Sixth Dynasties Thot, Set, Horus, and other gods were recognised as having KAS; that is to say, each was supposed to be possessed of his own Personality in addition to himself.* It was believed that the divine KA, this image which had the greater likeness to man, stood nearer to man than the god himself, and hence in the case of votive stelæ dedicated to the incarnation of Ptah in the sacred Apis-bull of Memphis, prayer for the divine favour and blessings is not as a rule addressed to the Apis, but to its KA. It is a very remarkable fact that in several inscriptions † the god

* We find occasional mention of the KA of the East and the KA of the West (WILKINSON, *Manners and Customs*, 2nd ed., III., pp. 200, 201), which are to be considered as being the KAS of the deities of the East and of the West, and not as KAS of the abstract conceptions of East and West.

† LEPSIUS, *Denkmäler*, III. 194, 1. 13; DÜMICHEN, *Tempel-inschriften*, I., pl. 29; VON BERGMANN, *Hierogl. Insch.*, pl. 33 pl. 61, col. 2; RENOUF, *Transactions of the Society of Biblical*

Rā is credited with no less than seven BAS and fourteen KAS, corresponding to the various qualities or attributes pertaining to his own being, and which he could communicate to the person of the king; such as: wealth, stability, majesty, glory, might, victory, creative power, etc.*

Thus the apprehension of the KA, of a man's Personality, as his *Doppelgänger*, or *Double*, found even in some of the oldest texts, acquired a far-reaching significance which extended not only to the doctrine of human immortality but also to the conception of the relations of gods to men.

As we have already stated, each man had a KA so long as he was alive, but at his death it left him and led an independent existence. Only after long wanderings did he meet it again in the world to come, and we still possess the prayer with which he was to greet it, beginning with the words, "Hail to thee who wast my KA during life! I come unto thee," etc.†

Archæology, VI., pp. 504 *et seq.*; BRUGSCH, *Dictionary, Supplt.*, pp. 997 *et seq.*, 1230.

* Cf. 1 Chron. xxix. 11, 12; Isa. xi. 2.

† This prayer is contained in that part of *The Book of the Dead*, chap. cv., entitled *Chapter whereby the KA of a person is satisfied in the Nether world*: "Hail to thee who wast my KA during life! Lo! I come unto thee, I arise resplendent, I labour, I am strong, I am hale (*var.*, I pass on), I bring grains of incense,

The second immortal part of man was his heart
(𓏤 𓂙 𓄣 *ǎb*).* The heart was removed from the body
by the embalmers, and the texts give no definite explanation as to what became of it. During certain

I am purified thereby, I purify thereby that which goeth forth
from thee. This conjuration of evil which I say; this warding
off of evil which I perform; (this conjuration) is not made
against me (?)" The conjuration runs as follows: "I am that
amulet of green felspar, the necklace of the god Rā, which is
given (*var.*, which I gave) unto them who are upon the horizon.
They flourish, I flourish, my KA flourishes even as they, my
duration of life flourishes even as they, my KA has abundance
of food even as they. The scale of the balance rises, Truth
rises high to the nose of the god Rā in that day on which my
KA is where I am (?) My head and my arm are made (?) to
where I am (?) I am he whose eye seeth, whose ears hear;
I am not a beast of sacrifice. The sacrificial formulæ proceed
where I am, for the upper ones "—otherwise said, "for the upper
ones of heaven." The funerary papyrus of Sûtimes (NAVILLE,
Todtenbuch, I., pl. 117) contains the following addition at the
end of this chapter: " I enter (?) unto thee (to the KA?).
I am pure, the Osiris is justified against his enemies." The
accompanying vignette for this chapter shows the deceased
as worshipping or sacrificing before the KA-sign on a standard.
Occasionally we find the KA sign represented as enclosing
pictures of offerings, a form explained by the common double
meaning of the word KA, which signifies both "*Double*" and *food*.

* In the religious texts the heart is called both 𓏤 𓂙 𓄣 𓏤 *ǎb*,
and 𓂝 𓄣 *ḥāti*. Sometimes, as in *The Book of the Dead*,
chap. xxvi. *et seq.*, the two were differentiated; but, generally
speaking, the two terms appear to have been synonymous.

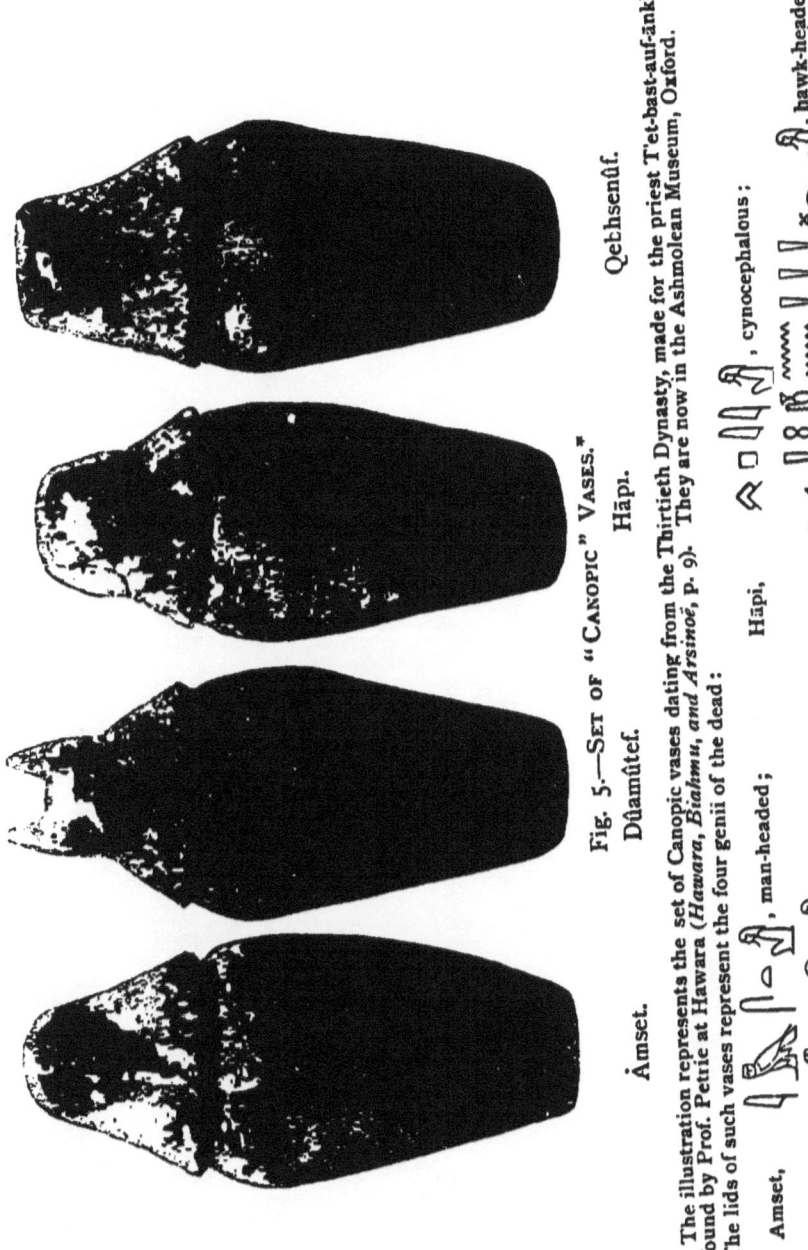

Àmset.   Dûamûtef.   Hâpi.   Qebhsenûf.

Fig. 5.—Set of "Canopic" Vases.*

* The illustration represents the set of Canopic vases dating from the Thirtieth Dynasty, made for the priest T'et-bast-auf-ânkh, and found by Prof. Petrie at Hawara (*Hawara, Biahmu, and Arsinoë*, p. 9). They are now in the Ashmolean Museum, Oxford.

The lids of such vases represent the four genii of the dead:

Àmset,   [hieroglyphs] , man-headed ;

Dûamûtef,   [hieroglyphs] , jackal-headed ;

Hâpi,   [hieroglyphs] , cynocephalous ;

Qebhsenûf,   [hieroglyphs] , hawk-headed.

periods of Egyptian history, but still comparatively
rarely, it was enclosed, as were the rest of the viscera,
in special alabaster, limestone, or wooden vases, of
which four were placed with the mummy in its grave.
These vases are generally but most erroneously called
"Canopic" vases. They usually date from the times
of the New Empire, but we have some few dating
from the Ancient Empire. In other cases the viscera
were replaced within the body after its embalmment,
and with them waxen images of the four genii of
the dead as their guardian divinities. But for the
most part documents do not afford us any informa-
tion as to what was done with the material heart.
Perhaps the priests took measures for its disappear-
ance in order to furnish some tangible foundation
for their doctrine concerning the heart. Certain
statements of Greek writers seem to imply some
such proceeding. According to these authorities the
viscera, which must have included the heart, were
cast into the Nile, because they were designated as
the source of all human error. Porphyry gives us
even the form of the prayer which was repeated
when the chest containing the intestines was presented before the Sun; and if the text of this
prayer has not hitherto been confirmed from original

documents it is yet so thoroughly Egyptian in character that its authenticity cannot be doubted.*

* PLUTARCH, *Septem sap. conviv.*, p. 159 B: "We then, said
I" (Diales), "render these tributes to the belly (τῇ γαστρί). But
if Solon or any one else has any allegation to make we will
listen." "By all means," said Solon, "lest we should appear
more senseless than the Egyptians, who cutting up the dead
body showed [the entrails] to the sun, then cast them into the
river, but of the rest of the body, as now become pure, they
took care.   For in reality this [the belly] is the pollution of our
flesh, and the Hell, as in Hades,—full of dire streams, and of
wind and fire confused together, and of dead things."

PLUTARCH, *De esu carnium orat.*, ii., p. 996, 38: "As the
Egyptians, taking out from the dead the belly (τὴν κοιλίαν) and
cutting it up before the sun, cast it away, as the cause of all
the sins which the man has committed ; in like manner that we
ourselves, cutting out gluttony and bloodthirstiness, should purify
the rest of our life."

PORPHYRY, *De abst.*, iv., 10: "When they embalm those of
the noble that have died, together with their other treatment of
the dead body, they take out the belly (τὴν κοιλίαν), and put
it into a coffer, and holding the coffer to the sun they protest, one
of the embalmers making a speech on behalf of the dead.   This
speech, which Euphantus translated from his native language,
is as follows: "O Lord, the Sun, and all ye gods who give life
to men, receive me and make me a companion to the eternal
gods.   For the gods, whom my parents made known to me,
as long time as I have had my life in this world I have continued
to reverence, and those who gave birth to my body I have ever
honoured.   And for the rest of men, I have neither slain any,
nor defrauded any of anything entrusted to me, nor committed
any other wicked act, but if I haply in my life have sinned at

But the immortal heart of a man, which stood in a similar relationship to his material heart as his KA to the whole body, left him at death and journeyed on alone through the regions of the other world till it reached the " Abode of Hearts."   Its first meeting with the deceased to whom it had belonged was in the Hall of Judgment, where it stood forth as his accuser ; for in it all his good and evil thoughts had found expression during his lifetime.   They had not originated there, for the heart was essentially divine and pure, but it had of necessity harboured and known them,* and therefore it was called upon to testify concerning the man's former thoughts and deeds before Osiris, judge of the dead.

In the meantime the mummy was without heart, and had become lifeless and dead ; for to pierce the heart of anything was equivalent to utterly destroying

all, by either eating or drinking what was unlawful, not on my own account did I sin, but on account of these (showing the coffer in which the belly [ἡ γαστήρ] lay)."   And having said these things he throws it into the river ; but the rest of the body, as pure, he embalms.   Thus they thought that they needed to excuse themselves to the Deity on account of what they had eaten and drunk, and therefore to reproach the belly."

* It was in this sense that the Egyptians regarded the heart as the seat of the feelings, and spoke of the heart as rejoicing, as mourning, as weeping.

it. The OSIRIS, too (to which we shall presently return), would have shared the fate of the mummy had the device not been conceived of providing the latter with an artificial heart in place of its own original one, which had returned to the gods. The provisional heart was represented by an artificial

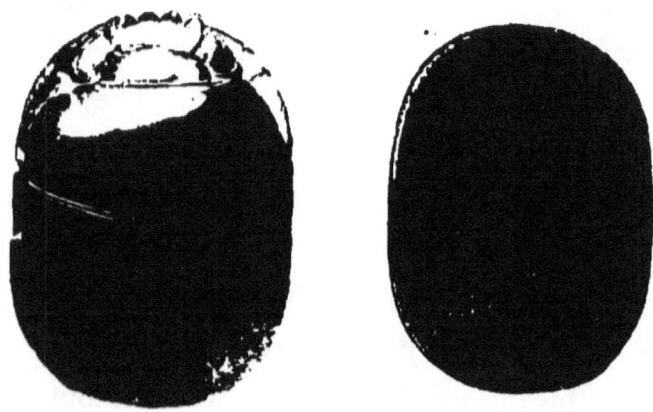

Fig. 6.—A heart scarab.*

scarabæus, generally made of hard greenish stone in the image of the beetle, which was a symbol of genesis and resurrection (fig. 6). Underneath it was made flat, and inscribed with magic formulæ,† that it might be the substitute for the dead man's heart,

* The illustration is taken from photographs of a scarab in the Edwards collection at University College, London.

† For the translation of chap. xxx b. of *The Book of the Dead*, which formed the usual inscriptions on heart scarabs, see p. 53.

and also ensure his resurrection by virtue of its form. But when his own heart was restored to him the scarabæus lost its significance. Like all the rest of the amulets which the Egyptians gave to their dead, its efficacy only availed for the space of time intervening between death and the reunion of those

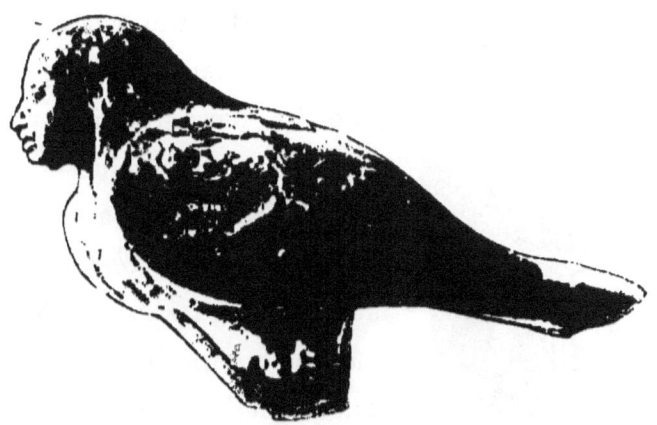

Fig. 7.—The Ba as a bird.

elements which death had separated. When once the resurrection had taken place there was no further need of amulets, nor any hurt through lack of them.

Another immortal part of man was the ⟨hieroglyph⟩, ⟨hieroglyph⟩, ⟨hieroglyph⟩, BA. This conception most nearly corresponds to our "soul," for it was a being which, on the death of the man in whom it had dwelt, left him in order to fly to the gods, to whom it was closely akin, and with whom it abode when not united to the man. But, nevertheless, the BA was neither immaterial nor able to dispense with food and drink.*   It bore the form of a human-headed bird (fig. 7), sometimes with hands (figs. 10, 14); or of a ram-headed scarabæus (fig. 8).   From the fifteenth to the eleventh century

Fig. 8.—Ram-headed scarabæus. †

B.C. it was preferably represented under the second form which is really nothing more than its hieroglyphic symbol. The phonetic value of the ram, is *ba*, and of the scarabæus, *kheper*, which latter means *to be, to become;* and the composite figure of the ram-headed scarabæus signifies, therefore, something like " he who has become a soul."

It is otherwise with the first image, which really represents the soul as it was imagined by the Egyptians. We have sculptured figures and drawings (fig. 9)

* The possession of the formula in chap. cxlviii. of *The Book of the Dead*, from line 8, ensured abundance (of food) to the BA of the dead.

† Illustrations 7 and 8 are taken from photographs of objects in the Edwards Museum at University College.

showing the little soul perched by the sarcophagus, touching the mummy, and bidding it farewell before rising to the gods.* In other scenes the soul is

Fig. 9.—The Ba visiting the mummy on its funeral couch. (*From "The Book of the Dead."*)

depicted as it comes flying from heaven with the sign of life in its hand, and approaching the grave

* See *The Book of the Dead*, NAVILLE'S edition, pls. 4, 97, 101, 104; LEPSIUS' edition, pls. 33, etc., etc.

to visit the mummy; or as flying down into the vault with the offerings which it had found at the door of the tomb, bringing bread in one hand and a jar of water in the other, as food and drink for the body which once invested it (fig. 10).

This conception of the soul as a kind of bird is noteworthy when compared with the ideas which other nations have formed of it. The Greeks sometimes represented the εἴδωλον, or soul, as a small winged human figure (fig. 11); in Roman times it was imagined as a butterfly (fig. 12); and in mediæval reliefs and pictures we see it leaving the mouth of the dead man as a child (fig. 13), or a little naked man.[*]

Fig. 10.—The Ba flying down the shaft of the tomb and bringing offerings to the mummy. (*From " The Book of the Dead."*)

[*] See, *e.g.*, illustration, and Orcagna's fresco of the Triumph of Death, in the Campo Santo of Pisa.

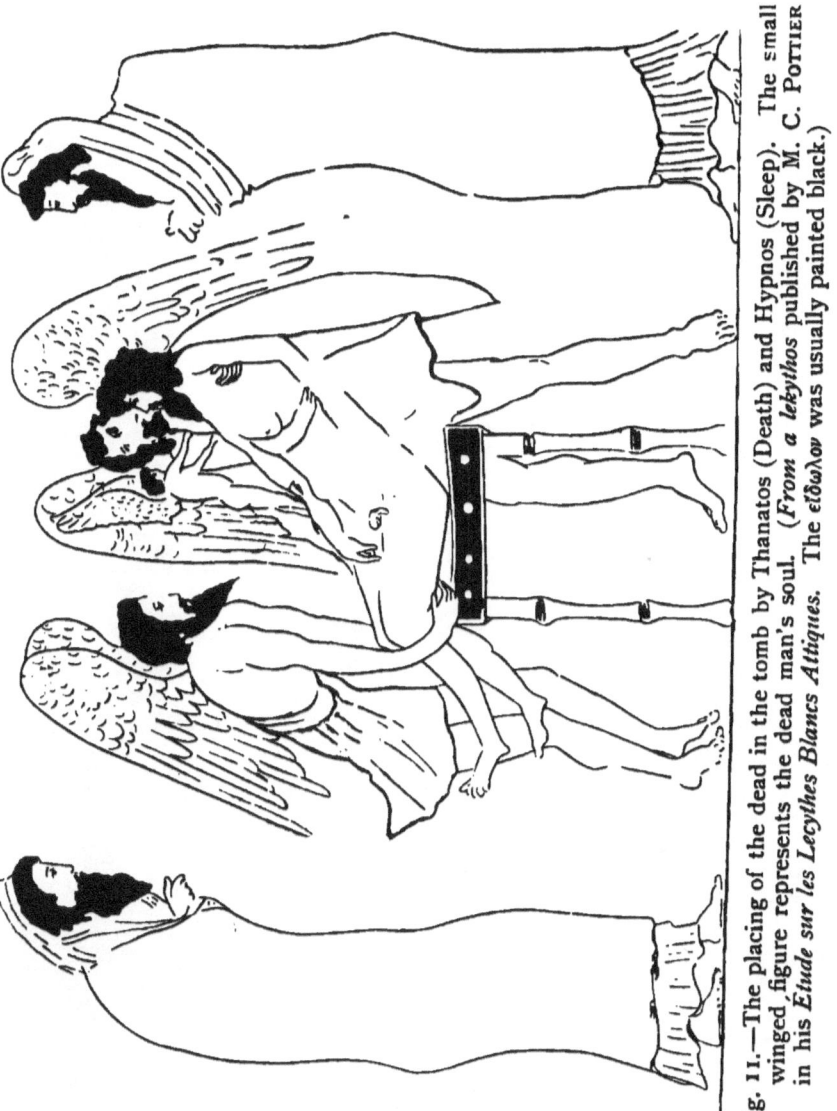

Fig. 11.—The placing of the dead in the tomb by Thanatos (Death) and Hypnos (Sleep). The small winged figure represents the dead man's soul. (*From a lekythos* published by M. C. POTTIER in his *Etude sur les Lecythes Blancs Attiques*. The εἴδωλον was usually painted black.)

Fig. 12.—Scene from a sculptured sarcophagus of the third century A.D., in the Capitoline Museum, Rome. To the left, below the chariot of Selene and the draped figure of Night, lies the dead body of the man, whose soul hovers above him as a butterfly beside the inverted torch of the pensive winged boy representing either Sleep or Death. Fate sits with open scroll at the dead man's head, and above her his soul is again represented as a Psyche, carried away by Hermes. (See BOTTARI, *Musée Capitoline*, vol. iv, pl. xxv. Cf. also many representations of Amor and Psyche in ancient art, showing Psyche—the soul—sometimes as a winged figure and sometimes as a butterfly.)

Fig. 13.—The soul of a man leaving him at his death in the form of a naked child, and received by an angel. (*From the porch of the cathedral church of St. Trophimus, at Arles.*)

The latter form recalls that of the Egyptian KA, although the idea which it embodies reminds one rather of the BA.

The ⸻ 𓏺𓀀𓆑𓏲𓏛, SĀHÛ, also was considered as immortal. This is invariably depicted as a swathed mummy, and represented the form which the- man wore upon earth. Originally it was related to the KA, but whereas the latter was a complete Personality, the SĀHÛ was nothing but a hull,—a form without contents. Yet this also was of the gods and imperishable, returning to its heavenly home when death had set it free. Since the body, or KHA,[*] had also the same form, it naturally came about that when the mummy was mentioned in religious texts as reanimated by the KA it was frequently confounded with the SĀHÛ. In this sense it is said that "the SĀHÛ lives in the Sarcophagus (or in the underworld), it grows (*rûd*), it renews itself (*renp*)." [†] But in more precise texts the two things are kept distinct, as, *e.g.*, "the BA (soul) sees its KHA, it rests upon its SĀHÛ.[‡] At such times the BA had power

[*] See p. 10.

[†] VON BERGMANN, *Sarkophag des Panehemisis*, I., pp. 11, 15, 24; PIERRET, *Insc. du Louvre*, II., p. 23; MARIETTE, *Dendérah*, iv., 62*a*.

[‡] *The Book of the Dead*, lxxxix. 6.

over the SĀHÛ, and, as is said on the Sarcophagus
of Panehemisis, "the SĀHÛ lives at the command
of the BA." *

In close connection with the SĀHÛ was the
𓀭𓅓𓇋𓏌𓂝𓇳, KHAÏB, the shadow, represented
as a fan, or sunshade (fig. 14), in scenes professing
to portray the next world. †

As all earthly forms must needs have their
shadows, such was also the case with things in the
world to come ; there, too, the sun shone and all
the optical phenomena of earth were repeated. But,
not content to accept this as a simple fact, the
Egyptians ascribed separate existences both to the
shadows of the dead and to those of gods and genii.
According to Egyptian belief a shadow might live on
independently, apart from its owner, and this was
exactly what it was supposed to do at the moment
when death had taken place ; then the KHAÏB went
forth alone to appear in the realm of the gods.
This Ancient Egyptian idea of the independent
existence of a man's shadow recalls to our minds

* VON BERGMANN, *Sarkophag des Panehemisis*, I., p. 37, where
the translation is not quite accurately given.   ·

† In *Transactions of the Society of Biblical Archæology*, VIII.,
p. 386 *et seq.*, BIRCH has collected passages bearing on this
point.

Chamisso's story of Peter Schlemihl, published in 1823.*

The KA, the ÀB, the BA, the SĀHÛ, and the KHAÏB constituted the chief elements of that which was immortal in man, but others were also occasionally included, especially one which was called the KHÛ,

Fig. 14.—BA and KHAÏB.   (*From "The Book of the Dead."*)

, *i.e.* the Luminous.† To these, however, there is less frequent reference ; they were of import-

---

* On primitive beliefs as to a man's shadow being a vital part of himself, see FRAZER, *The Golden Bough*, Vol. I., pp. 141-44.

† See MASPERO, *Recueil de Travaux relatifs à l'Égypt*, III., p. 105 *et seq.*; and *Histoire Ancienne des Peuples de l'Orient*, Vol. I., p. 114. In *The Book of the Dead*, chap. lxxxix., 3, the KHÛ is mentioned in connection with the BA ; in chap. cxlix., 40, with the KHAÏB ; and in chap. xcii., 5, with both.

ance in local cults only, and were either included among the parts already mentioned or were so vaguely defined that they may be safely left out of account in treating of the soul as conceived by the Egyptians without danger of our conception being falsified by the omission.

When the immortal was thus resolved into its component parts at death, what then became of the human individuality which had resulted from their combined action, and how could its different parts find each other again in the next world, in order to form the new man of the resurrection? The Egyptians had evolved a very simple solution of this problem, although one which, according to our mode of thought, stands in direct contradiction to their doctrine of the soul. It was assumed that in addition to his immortal elements the man as a person of a particular appearance and character was also endowed with a kind of deathlessness, which seems to have held good only for a time, and not for ever. To this conception of a dead man, in whom soul and life were lacking but who in the interim still possessed existence, feeling, and thought, the Egyptians gave the name of OSIRIS.

Osiris was the first divine King of Egypt who reigned in true human likeness; he civilised the Egyptians, instructed them in agriculture, gave them laws, and taught them true religion. After a long and blessed reign he fell a prey to the machinations of his brother Set (Typhon), and having been slain was constrained to descend into the underworld, where he evermore lived and reigned as judge and king of the dead. His fate of death was the fate of all men. Every one, when his earthly pilgrimage was ended, must descend into the underworld by the gates of death; but each man hoped to rise again, even as Osiris had risen, to lead henceforth the life of the blessed. In this hope men called their dead OSIRIS, just as Germans speak of their dead as "blessed,"—hoping that blessedness may indeed be their lot. Death had not changed Osiris; as he had been king on earth, so he was king in the world beyond death. In the same way man, too, remained that which he had been here; death merely made a break in his life, without altering any of his conditions of existence.

The relation subsisting between a man's OSIRIS and his mummy was not clearly apprehended, even by the Egyptians themselves. Identical they were not—that fact is obviously implied by the texts, which never once substitute the mummy for the OSIRIS; men knew also from experience that no mummy had ever left its place of embalmment, or the tomb, to journey on into the next world.   Yet

Fig. 15.—Hypocephalus, from a drawing by Dr. W. H. Rylands.

mummy and OSIRIS were nevertheless not entirely different and distinct; both had the same appearance and the same character.   Moreover, the texts describe the OSIRIS as resembling the mummy in appearance while really differing from it, and the embalmers equipped the mummy as though it were called upon

to journey forth as the OSIRIS.   The inherent contradiction in all this arose principally from the fact
that the Egyptian hoped and believed that shortly
after death he would arise again, complete in flesh
and blood as he had lived upon earth ; whereas
experience contradicted his creed, for it showed him
that the mummy never did and never could leave the
earth.   He extricated himself from the dilemma by
providing the mummy with a *Doppelgänger* : its own
perfect counterpart, yet not itself.   When once we
have familiarised ourselves with this singular idea
we find in it a simple key to all the riddles of
the OSIRIS.

The mummy was provided with an artificial heart
in the shape of a scarabæus,* because the OSIRIS
could not live without one, and also with various
amulets, by virtue of every one of which demons of
the next world could be overcome.   A stuccoed disc
of papyrus, linen, or bronze, which, by the figures and
formulæ inscribed upon it, had mystic power to preserve the needful warmth of life to the Osiris (fig. 15),
was placed under the head of the mummy.†   The soles

---

* See p. 30.

† A certain part in the religious life of our own time has been
played by a similar " Hypocephalus," viz., the Mormon Scriptures

of the feet which had trodden the mire of earth were removed in order that the OSIRIS might tread the Hall of Judgment with pure feet; and the gods were prayed to grant milk to the OSIRIS that he might bathe his feet in it and so assuage the pain which the removal of the soles must needs have caused him.   And, finally, the soles which had been excised were placed within the mummy in order that the OSIRIS might find them to hand for the completion of his Personality.*   That nothing might be wanting to this Personality, the gods were besought that the mummy should not suffer earthly corruption, and it was held to be of supreme importance that flesh and bones, muscles and limbs should all remain in place. With the mummy were also placed *The Book of the Dead,* as well as other religious and mystic texts needed by the OSIRIS for his guidance through the regions beyond the grave, and from which he might learn the prayers which had to be spoken in due order and place according to strict prescriptions.   In short,

(cf. JOSEPH SMITH, *A Pearl of Great Price,* 1851, p. 7).   For particulars of the Hypocephalus of the illustration see *Proceedings of the Society of Biblical Archæology,* Vol. VI., p. 52, and plate.

* See EBERS, *Æg. Zeitschr.,* 1867, p. 108; 1871, p. 48; WIEDEMANN, *Proceedings of the Orientalist Congress at St. Etienne,* II., p. 155.

the mummy was treated precisely as though it were an OSIRIS. But the difference was great: the mummy remained within the sarcophagus in the sepulchral chamber, while the OSIRIS proceeded on his way.

The journey of the OSIRIS, treated at wearisome length, forms the favourite subject of Egyptian texts, and to this is devoted the largest and best known work in the religious literature of the nation: the compilation called by us *The Book of the Dead.* This book contains no systematic account of the journey, such as the analogy of similar literatures might lead us to expect, but exhibits it in a series of disconnected stages by giving the prayers which the OSIRIS must repeat when passing through different parts of the underworld, or on encountering certain genii there. A chapter is devoted to each prayer, but the chapters do not follow each other in the order in which the prayers were to be used. The Egyptians never attained to any clear idea of the Osirian underworld; the same confusion and obscurity reigned over it as over their whole conception of the unseen world and of deity. They pondered deeply over a series of separate problems without being able to unite the results into one consistent whole, which should command acceptance, or to form any definite and permanent topography of the regions beyond the tomb. Hence there is no fixed sequence for the chapters of *The Book of the Dead*; the order varies materially in the different manuscripts to which we are indebted for our knowledge of the work. The number of chapters in the different copies also varies; while in some it is small, in others, as in the Ptolemaic copy for a certain Aûfānkh, published by Lepsius, it reaches to one hundred and sixty-five. Since there was no fixed rule as to order or number, priest or scribe might make a selection of such chapters as he or the family of the deceased held to be the most essential, and each was at liberty to form for himself a more or less modified conception of the characteristics of the underworld.

We cannot here follow the OSIRIS through all the details of his journey, but must be content to know that according to the account in *The Book of the Dead* he issued victorious from all his trials, overcame all enemies whom he encountered, and was ushered at length into the Hall of the Double Truth, and received by the goddess of Truth. Here also he found the chief gods of the Osirian cycle gathered together, and the forty-two assessors of Divine Justice near the canopy under which the god Osiris was enthroned. Then the deceased spoke, and proceeded to recite the " Negative Confession "—a denial of sins of commission—declaring that he had not been guilty of certain definite sins, and denying one or another particular form of guilt to each of the assessors. He had not done evil, had not robbed, nor murdered, nor lied, not caused any to weep, not injured the property of the gods, and so on.*

---

* The " Negative Confession " forms chap. cxxv. of *The Book of the Dead,* and varies slightly in different copies. The following is RENOUF's translation of the chapter as it appears in a Nineteenth Dynasty papyrus (see *The Papyrus of Ani,* London, 1890):—" I am not a doer of what is wrong. I am not a plunderer. I am not a robber. I am not a slayer of men. I do not stint the quantity of corn. I am not a niggard. I do not seize the property of the gods. I am not a teller of lies. I am not a monopoliser of food. I am no extortioner. I am not unchaste. I am not the cause of others' tears. I am not a dissembler. I am not a doer of violence. I am not of domineering character. I do not pillage cultivated land. I am not an eavesdropper. I am not a chatterer. I do not dismiss a case through self-interest. I am not unchaste with women or men. I am not obscene. I am not an exciter of alarms. I am not hot in speech. I do not turn a deaf ear to the words of righteousness. I am not foul-mouthed. I am not a striker. I am not a quarreller. I do not revoke my purpose. I do not multiply clamour in reply to words. I am not evil-minded or a doer of evil. I am not a reviler of the

The judges heard all in silence, giving no sign either of approval or disapproval; but when the confession was ended the heart of the deceased was brought forward and laid in the scales against the

Fig. 16.—The weighing of the dead man's heart against the feather symbolic of Maāt, the goddess of Truth. (*From " The Book of the Dead."*)

image or symbol óf Truth. The weighing was superintended by the gods Anubis and Horus,

king. I put no obstruction upon the water. I am not a bawler. I am not a reviler of the God. 1 am not fraudulent. I am not sparing in offerings to the gods. I do not deprive the dead of the funeral cakes. I do not take away the cakes of the child, or profane the god of my locality. I do not kill sacred animals,"

while Thot, the scribe of the gods, stood by ready
to record the result (fig. 16).*

This was the time for the deceased anxiously to
call upon his heart in the prescribed formula from
The Book of the Dead,† not to bear witness

---

* On the Egyptian Goddess of Truth, see WIEDEMANN, *La
Déesse Maā,* in the *Annales du Musée Guimet,* x., pp. 561 *et
seq.* With regard to the meaning of the Egyptian name and
word *Maāt,* which is generally translated "truth, or justice,"
Renouf has said : "The Egyptians recognised a divinity in those
cases only where they perceived the presence of a fixed Law,
either of permanence or change. The earth abides for ever,
and so do the heavens. Day and night, months, seasons, and
years succeed each other with unfailing regularity ; the stars
are not less constant in their course, some of them rising and
setting at fixed intervals, and others eternally circling round
the pole in an order which never is disturbed. This *regularity,*
which is the constitutive character of the Egyptian divinity, was
called ⸻ *Maāt.* The gods were said to be *nebû maāt,*
'possessors of *maāt,*' or *ânchiû em maāt,* 'subsisting by or
through *maāt.*' *Maāt* is in fact the Law and Order by which
the universe exists. Truth and justice are but forms of *Maāt* as
applied to human action."—*Papyrus of Ani, Introduction,* p. 2.

† This prayer is contained in chap. xxx. of *The Book of the
Dead* :—

"*Chapter whereby the heart of a person is not kept back from
him in the Netherworld.*

Heart mine which is that of my mother,
Whole heart mine which is that of my birth,
Let there be no estoppel against me through evidence, let no

against him, for "the heart of a man is his own god," * and must now determine his everlasting fate. If his heart were content with him, and the scales turned in his favour, then the god Thot commanded that his heart should be restored to him to be set again in its place. This was done, and forthwith the immortal elements which death had separated began to reunite. His KA, and all the remaining parts of himself, were now restored to the justified OSIRIS, who was thus built up into the complete man who had once walked the earth, and who now entered upon a new life, the ever-lasting life of the righteous and the blessed. He

> hindrance be made to me by the divine Circle; fall thou not against me in presence of him who is at the Balance.
> Thou art my genius (KA), who art by me (in my KHA-T), the Artist who givest soundness to my limbs.
> Come forth to the bliss towards which we are bound;
> Let not those Ministrants who deal with a man according to the course of his life give a bad odour to my name.
> Pleasant for us, pleasant for the listener, is the joy of the Weighing of the Words.
> Let not lies be uttered in presence of the great god, Lord of the Amenti.
> Lo! how great art thou (as the triumphant one)."
> —*Renouf's translation.*

* As stated on the mummy case of Panehemisis, ed. VON BERGMANN, I., p. 29.

was joyfully admitted by the gods into their circle, and was henceforth as one of them.

The Book of the Dead, and cognate religious texts, always assume that judgment goes in favour of the deceased, that his heart approves him, and that he becomes one of the blessed. Nowhere are we clearly informed as to the fate of the condemned who could not stand before the god Osiris. We are told that the enemies of the gods perish, that they are destroyed or overthrown ; but such vague expressions afford no certainty as to how far the Egyptians in general believed in the existence of a hell as a place of punishment or purification for the wicked ;[*] or whether, as seems more probable, they held some general belief that when judgment was pronounced against a man his heart and other immortal parts were not restored to him. For such a man no re-edification and no resurrection was possible. The immortal elements were divine, and by nature pure and imperishable ; but they could be preserved

[*] The conception of a kind of hell is certainly found in the book *Am Dûat* (cf. JÉQUIER, *Le livre de ce qu'il y a dans l'Hadès*, Paris, 1894, p. 127); such allusions are, however, exceptional, and Egyptian belief in a hell appears to have existed at times only, and to have been confined to certain classes of society.

from entering the OSIRIS, from re-entering the hull of the man who had proved himself unworthy of them. The soul, indeed, as such did not die, although personal annihilation was the lot of the evil-doer in whom it had dwelt. But it was the hope of continued individuality which their doctrine held out to the Egyptians ; this it was which they

Fig. 17.—The Blessed Dead ploughing and sowing by the waters of the celestial Nile. (*From " The Book of the Dead."*)

promised to the good and in all probability denied to the wicked.

After judgment the righteous entered into blessed-ness, unchanged in appearance as in nature ; the only difference being that, while the existence which they had led upon earth had been limited in its duration, the life of the world to come was eternal. But the future blessedness for which the Egyptian

hoped was far from being a passive state of bliss
such as is promised by most of the higher religions,

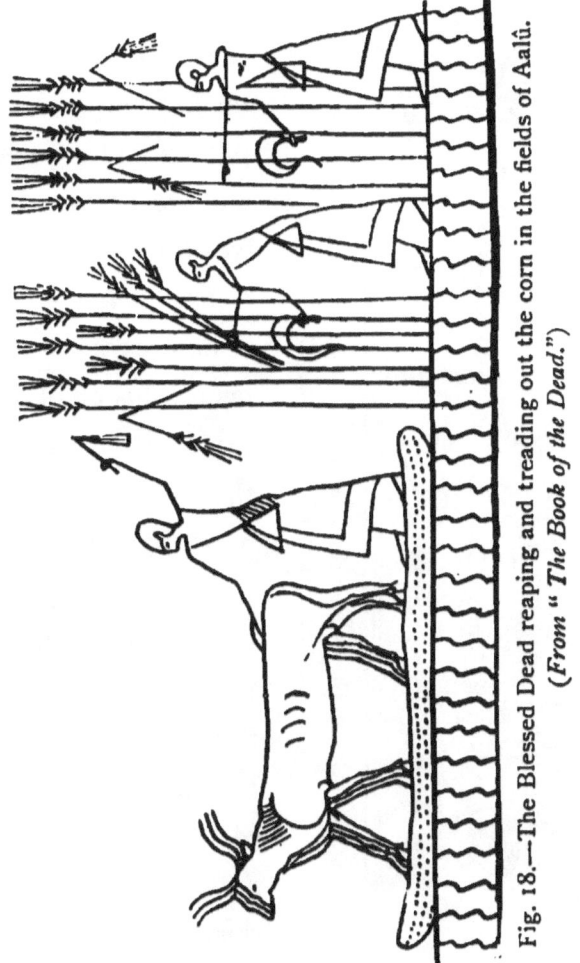

Fig. 18.—The Blessed Dead reaping and treading out the corn in the fields of Aalû.
(*From "The Book of the Dead."*)

an absorption into the All or into the Godhead, a
dreamy state of floating in everlasting repose, content,
and unimpassioned joy. The average Egyptian

expected to lead as active a life in the world
to come as he had led
here.   Although with
the Godhead, he counted
on retaining his inde-
pendent individuality in
all   respects   and   on
working   and   enjoying
himself even as he had
done on earth.   He ex-
pected his chief employ-
ment to be agriculture,
the   occupation   which
must have seemed most
natural to a people al-
most entirely dependent
upon   the   produce   of
the   fields.   A vignette
belonging to chap. cx.
of *The Book of the
Dead* represents   the
dead at work in the

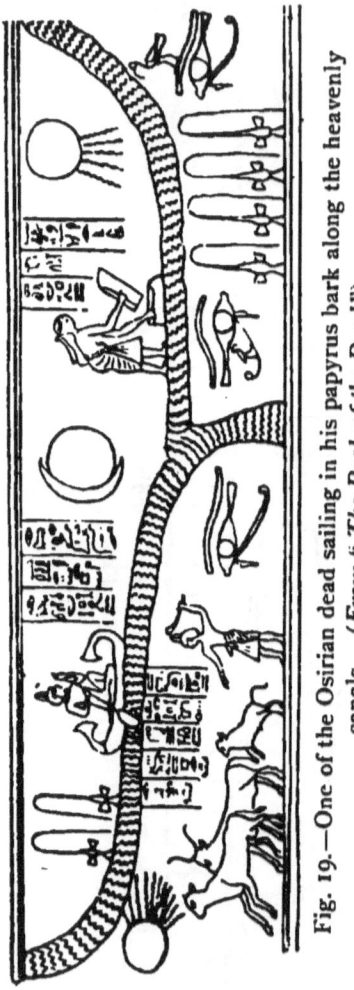

Fig. 19.—One of the Osirian dead sailing in his papyrus bark along the heavenly canals. (*From " The Book of the Dead."*)

fields of the Blessed,* ploughing with oxen, casting

* The "fields of Aalû"; cf. the "Elysian fields" of the
Greeks.

the seed-corn into the furrows (fig. 17), cutting the ripe ears with sickles, driving oxen to tread out the grain from the straw (fig. 18), and finally piling up the corn in heaps against it was required to serve for the making of bread. For change and

Fig. 20.—The Blessed Dead making offerings to the celestial Nile-god.
(*From " The Book of the Dead."*)

recreation they sailed upon the canals of the next world in their boats (fig. 19), played at draughts with their own souls, or made offerings to the gods, especially to the celestial Nile, which gave water to their fields and fertility to their seed (fig. 20). All went on exactly as here, excepting that the work of the blessed was invariably crowned with success. The Nile always overflowed the fields to best advantage, the corn grew five ells high and its ears were two ells long, the harvest never failed to be abundant, the weather was always favourable, the fresh and pleasant north wind was always blowing, the foe was always conquered, and the gods graciously accepted all offerings and requited the givers with rich gifts of all kinds. In short, the life of the dead in the kingdom of the gods was an idealised earthly life, although not always a very moral life according to our standards.

But this belief in the life of the next world as the exact counterpart of this implied a danger which involved the Egyptian in heavy cares. The dead lived, therefore they must of necessity eat and drink, for without these processes the continuation of life was inconceivable; if the dead were without food they would be starved. The inscription of the sepulchral pyramid of Ûnas, an Egyptian king of the Fifth Dynasty, gives expression to this fear. "Evil is it for Ûnas," says that text, "to be hungry and have nothing to eat; evil is it for Ûnas to be thirsty and have nothing to drink." The necessities of life were, indeed, partly ensured to the dead by means of the offerings made to them by their sur-

vivors on recurrent feast-days, and partly mysteriously
created for their use in the next world by the repeti-
tion of magic formulæ in this.* But if the offerings

Fig. 21.—Ancient kingdom KA-statues of servants—potters and
bread-makers. (*Originals in the Ghizeh Museum.*)

ceased, or if no one took the trouble to repeat the
formulæ, the dead were left to their own resources,
and must work, and till the land, and earn their
own living.

* See p. 19.

Such enforced labour could hardly have appeared very attractive to Egyptians of the upper classes, and so an expedient suggested by the conditions of their earthly life was devised for evading it on their behalf. The rich man who had servants to work for him in this world was desirous of securing like service for himself in the world to come. In the time of the Ancient Empire it seems to have been taken for granted that those who were servants in this life would be servants also in the life beyond. With this selfish end in view the rich of those times had placed within their own sepulchral chambers KA-statues of their servants in order to ensure immortal life to them also (fig. 21). As the old Germans were followed into the next world by their slaves and horses; as other uncivilised nations sent the servants of the dead to the realm of death after their masters,* so in

* From scenes in the tomb of Mentûherkhepeshf at Thebes, dating from the beginning of the Nineteenth Dynasty, we have evidence that Egyptian funeral ceremonies occasionally included human sacrifice at the gate of the tomb, the object of such sacrifice being doubtless that of sending servants to the dead. But the practice would seem to have been very exceptional, at any rate after Egypt had entered upon her long period of greatness. See MASPERO, *Mémoires de la Mission Archéologique du Caire*, V., p. 452; cf. WIEDEMANN, in *Le Muséon*, XIII., p. 457 *et seq.*; see also GRIFFITH, *The Tomb of Paheri*, pp. 20, 21, in the Eleventh Memoir of the Egypt Exploration Fund.

Ancient Egypt a certain portion of mankind was set apart to serve the rest through all eternity. But as Egyptian civilisation advanced and a more humane state of feeling dawned, these views were modified, and the thought gained ground that all Egyptians were equal in the presence of death and of the gods. So the rich man was obliged to renounce his hope of finding his servants again at his service beyond the tomb, and was face to face with the old fear of being reduced to heavy toil through the possible negligence of his successors.

A most singular expedient was adopted to avert this danger : little images of clay, or wood, or stone, or even of bronze, were made in human likeness, inscribed with a certain formula,* and placed within the tomb, in the hope that they would there attain to life and become the useful servants of the blessed dead ; they are the so-called ÛSHABTIÛ (or Respondents), of which hundreds and thousands of specimens

* Chapter vi. of *The Book of the Dead* consists of this formula, which there reads: "O Ûshabti there ! Should I be called and appointed to do any of the labours that are done in the Netherworld by a person according to his abilities, lo ! all obstacles have been beaten down for thee ; be thou counted for me at every moment, for planting the fields, for watering the soil, for conveying the sands of East and West. Here am I, whithersoever thou callest me ! "—*Renouf's Translation.*

may be found in collections of Egyptian antiquities
(see Frontispiece *). These "servants for the underworld," or "servants to the OSIRIS," as the texts call
them, owed their very being and life to the dead, and
stood to him in the same relation as man to God.
And as men seek to testify their gratitude to the
Creator by doing Him service, so it was hoped that
these little figures would show their thankfulness by
their diligence, and spare their master and maker
all toil.

Many other customs arose out of similar ideas to
those which gave rise to the institution of ÛSHABTIÛ.
Articles of personal adornment and for toilet use,
wreaths, weapons, carriages, playthings, and tools
were given to the dead, and a whole set of household
furniture was often laid away in the grave in order
that the OSIRIS should not be obliged to set to work
at once to make or collect these things for himself on
his entrance into the next world ; for this purpose
choice was often made of such objects as the man
had used and valued in his lifetime. All this care,

* The frontispiece represents one of 399 ÛSHABTIÛ made for a
priest named Horût'a, who lived during the Twenty-sixth Dynasty.
These USHABTIÛ were found at Hawara by Petrie : see *Kahun,
Gurob, and Hawara*, pp. 9, 19.

however, was bestowed not simply in the interest of those who had entered upon the life everlasting but also in that of those who were left behind. Among other powers possessed by the dead was that of going to and fro upon earth ; and, to prevent their exercise of it, all things whose lack might impel them to revisit the scenes of their earthly lives were placed within the tombs, for their visits might not be altogether pleasant for survivors withholding any part of the goods which belonged to the dead. But these facts must not lead us to conclude that the tomb was the permanent dwelling of the dead, and that the objects placed within it were really intended for his use there, and for all time.

As the amulets laid in and about the mummy were for the use of the OSIRIS, so the furniture and implements placed near the coffin were intended not so much for the mummy lying in its tomb as for the OSIRIS dwelling with the gods. Each of these objects had its heavenly counterpart, even as the mummy was represented by the OSIRIS.*

* Professor Petrie, speaking of his discovery that it was the Egyptian custom to place masonic deposits of miniature model tools, etc., underneath the foundations of temples, and giving an account of the foundation deposits which he found beneath the pyramid temple of Ûsertesen II., at Illahûn, says : "The reason

5

It was thus that the Egyptians sought to make themselves homes in the next world, and to secure all the comforts and pleasures of their earthly life in the life which was to come. Nevertheless, the pious Egyptian did not expect to remain for ever as an OSIRIS, or as a god in human likeness : he rather hoped for ever-increasing freedom, for the power of taking other shapes and transforming himself at will into quadrupeds ; or into birds—such as the swallow or the heron ; or into plants—more especially the lotus ; or even into gods.*

This is no doctrine of compulsory transmigration such as used to be freely ascribed to the Egyptians on the strength of the statements made by Hero-dotus † ; there is no question here of souls being

for burying such objects is yet unexplained ; but it seems not unlikely that they were intended for the use of the KAS of the builders, like the models placed in tombs for the KAS of the deceased. Whether each building had a KA, which needed ghostly repair by the builders' KAS, is also to be considered " (*Kahun, Gurob, and Hawara*, p. 22). We know that each building had its guardian spirit in the form of a serpent (cf. the representation of one dating from the time of Amenophis III., in Ghizeh, No. 217, published by MARIETTE, *Mon. Div.*, pl. 63 *b*).

* *The Book of the Dead*, chaps. lxxvi.—lxxxviii.

† " The Egyptians were also the first to broach the opinion that the soul of man is immortal, and that when the body dies it enters into an animal which is born at the same moment, thence

forced to assume fresh forms in which their purification is gradually worked out and their perfection achieved. To the Egyptian transmigration was not the doom of imperfect souls, but a privilege reserved for such as had already attained perfection. Again and again the texts assert that the blessed may assume any form and visit any place at will; body and place can no longer enthral him. He may travel round the heavens with the Sun-god Rā, or arise from the shades with Osiris in the "divine night" of the 26th of the month Khoiak (*i.e.* at the winter solstice); he is even as a god, nay, he is himself a god, able to live in and by Truth, actually taking it, indeed, as food and drink.

The power of the soul to incarnate itself at pleasure became one of the chief reasons for embalming the body. As we have seen, the preservation of the body was held to be necessary because the mummy

passing on (from one animal into another) until it has circled through all creatures of the earth, the water, and the air, after which it enters again into a new-born human frame. The whole period of the transmigration is (they say) three thousand years. There are Greek writers, some of an earlier, some of a later date, who have borrowed this doctrine from the Egyptians, and put it forward as their own."—HERODOTUS, II., 123. See WIEDEMANN, *Herodots Zweites Buch*, p. 457 *et seq.*

was supposed to be the material form of which the
OSIRIS was the essential reality.   But this temporary
need might have been met in simpler fashion, since
the journey of the Soul to the Hall of Judgment
was accomplished in a comparatively short time.
There was, however, a further need for which provision had to be made.   The soul might sometimes
visit the mummy, again take up its abode in its
former body, and, animating it anew, return to earth
under that form and thus revisit the spots where
once it had dwelt.   To this end it required an earthly
and tangible body, and this was supplied by the
mummy.   If the mummy were destroyed, then the
soul not only lost one of the forms in which it might
incarnate itself, but that one with which its interests
were naturally most closely connected—that one which
linked it to earth and best enabled it to exhort the
survivors to remember the funerary offerings, and to
see how it fared with those whom it had been obliged
to leave behind.   The destruction of the mummy
did not involve the destruction of the soul, but it
narrowed the soul's circle of activity and limited its
means of transmigration.

This doctrine gave rise to the necromantic theory
that a soul might be compelled by means of magic

formulæ to re-enter its body, and to speak through the dead lips. The magician who had brought this about could then stipulate for all kinds of favours before restoring the soul to freedom. It is true that such an attempt was reckoned highly dangerous; and, according to a tale dating from Ptolemaic times, a royal prince named Setna,* who had succeeded in the undertaking, paid heavily for having sought to make the spirits of the dead subject to him, when, through his own imprudence, he was overpowered by those whom he had invoked.

The above sketch of the eschatology of the Ancient Egyptians is drawn from their own religious texts. As to the origin of that system and the transformations which it had undergone before reaching the form under which it is known to us we are as yet entirely ignorant; but it is obvious that it must have developed gradually and assimilated many originally heterogeneous doctrines. For instance, the KA and the OSIRIS must surely once have had the same significance, and not have been considered as two

* For the "Story of Setna" see Vol. II. of Professor Petrie's *Egyptian Tales.*

different factors of the dead man's being until time
had brought about the fusion of two theological
systems—in one of which the KA was regarded as
the spiritual *Doppelgänger*, or Double, while in the
other it was named the OSIRIS. All attempts
at solving these and similar problems connected
with this subject are, as yet, mere hypotheses.
As far back as Egyptian history has been traced
the people appear to have been in possession not
only of written characters, national art and insti-
tutions, but also of a complete system of religion.
As in all other departments of Egyptian life and
thought, so with the Egyptian religion—we cannot
trace its beginnings. In the earliest glimpse of it
afforded by the Egyptian texts it appears as perfect
in all its essential parts; nor were after-times able
to effect much change in it by the addition of new
features. What greatly intensifies the deep historical
interest of Egyptian eschatology is that it testifies
not only to the fact that a whole nation believed in
the immortality of the soul four thousand years before
the birth of Christ, but also that this nation had
even then succeeded in clearly picturing the future
life to themselves after a fashion which may indeed
often seem strange and incomprehensible to modern

minds but to which we cannot deny a certain consistency and a deep spiritual connotation.

We shall not here discuss the many analogies subsisting between Egyptian belief and the religious systems of other nations and times, nor yet its great differences from them; and it is for the sciences of anthropology and comparative religion to determine to what extent the Egyptian doctrine of immortality originated in Egypt itself, and how much was brought there by the Egyptians from the common home which they had shared with the Semites and Indo-europeans.

www.ingramcontent.com/pod-product-compliance
Lightning Source LLC
Chambersburg PA
CBHW030007030726
47499CB00008B/2933